Before I Leave

JESSIXA BAGLEY

A NEAL PORTER BOOK
ROARING BROOK PRESS
NEW YORK

Copyright © 2016 by Jessixa Bagley

A Neal Porter Book

Published by Roaring Brook Press

Roaring Brook Press is a division of Holtzbrinck Publishing Holdings Limited Partnership

175 Fifth Avenue, New York, New York 10010

The art for this book was created with pen and watercolor on paper.

mackids.com

Library of Congress Cataloging-in-Publication Data

Bagley, Jessixa, author, illustrator.

Before I leave / Jessixa Bagley. — First edition.

pages cm

Summary: Leaving her best friend is difficult for a young hedgehog whose family is moving, but everyone assures her that things will be alright.

ISBN 978-1-62672-040-4 (hardcover)

1. Hedgehogs—Juvenile fiction. 2. Moving, Household—Juvenile fiction. 3. Friendship—Juvenile fiction. [1. Hedgehogs—Fiction. 2. Moving, Household—Fiction. 3. Friendship—Fiction.] I. Title.

PZ7.1.B3Be 2016

[E]—dc23

2015004009

Our books may be purchased in bulk for promotional, educational, or business use. Please contact your local bookseller or the Macmillan Corporate and Premium Sales Department at (800) 221-7945 ext. 5442 or by e-mail at MacmillanSpecialMarkets@macmillan.com.

First edition 2016

Book design by Jennifer Browne

Printed in China by RR Donnelley Asia Printing Solutions Ltd., Dongguan City, Guangdong Province

1 3 5 7 9 10 8 6 4 2

For Aaron—
my best friend for life

I found out we're moving.

Mom said I needed to pack.

She said you can't come with us.

And I don't want to go without you.

Before I leave . . .

. . . let's play!

One last time,

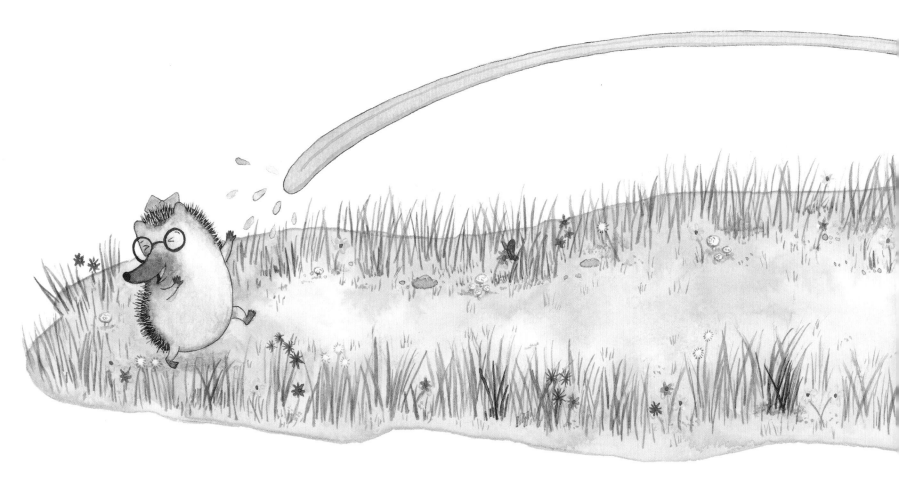

like nothing is changing.

I'll miss my old home, but Mom says our new home will be great.

I'll miss you and the fun we have together.

I'm scared to go.

But you say it will be okay,

and you'll see me soon.

But I'm not so sure.

You seem . . .

so far away . . .

. . . until I unpack,

and there you are!